Contents

1 ✦ Sherlock Holmes 1

2 ✦ The End? 8

3 ✦ The Box 17

4 ✦ The Visit 27

5 ✦ The Truth 38

6 ✦ The Unmasking 48

Chapter 1

Sherlock Holmes

Why is Sherlock Holmes the world's most famous detective? How did he change the world? It is now about a century after his last story. So why do groups of fans still meet to talk about his adventures? After all, he wasn't even a real person!

Holmes was invented by a Scottish writer named Arthur Conan Doyle. Doyle once studied under a professor named Dr. Joseph Bell. Bell was amazing. He could figure out a person's disease just by looking carefully at him or her. This gave Doyle the idea for a detective with the same ability. So in 1887 Holmes first appeared in the story "A Study in Scarlet."

Readers were immediately hooked. Why?

*First, of course, there were his astounding powers of observation. Holmes could look at people and instantly know things about them. Nothing was too tiny to escape his attention. He might see a shiny spot on a sleeve, for example, or a few bent blades of grass. To most these would mean nothing. But Holmes's keen eye would see worlds of meaning, laying open the dark secrets of criminals.

Then there was Holmes's great intellect. Today we use the hard drive, the screen, and the mouse to find information. Long before all this, Holmes's mind held a storehouse of facts that would help him solve crimes.

For example, other detectives always overlooked ashes. Left often at a crime scene, ashes from a cigar or pipe could be a key clue. Holmes made a careful study of ashes. He collected them, recorded everything about them, and learned to tell each bit* of ash apart from others. This knowledge helped him solve several very hard cases.

The way Holmes made light of his intellect made him all the more amazing to readers. His famous partner, Dr. John H. Watson, once named a street he had just left. Holmes told him all about the place—what shops were there, people he knew there, events that had happened there, and so forth. Flabbergasted, Watson asked how Holmes remembered all this. Holmes coolly replied he had taught himself everything about every single block in London, England!

Holmes was also a man of strange habits. Between cases he was lazy, quiet, and moody. Watson would often find him sunk in an easy chair and deep in thought, or playing the fiddle in the middle of the night, or just staring into space for hours on end, the tips of his long, slender fingers pressed together. This mood might last for weeks.

But once aroused to action, he became like a tiger! His long, lean body would uncoil like a spring. His eyes would shine with feverish intelligence. "Hurry, Watson," he would cry, "the game is afoot!" And like a tiger, he would never stop until the criminal was hunted down.

Most of the time, however, he never left his apartment, which was at 221 Baker Street. How did he know what was going on outside? He became friends with the city's poor children. These boys and girls—the "Baker Street Irregulars"—hung around the back streets and byways of London. They watched and listened. From them, Holmes learned things no ordinary detective could hope to know.

Disguises were another Holmes trademark. He could transform himself into almost anything—a broken-down old woman, a powerful weightlifter, or a grinning fool. Even Watson, his lifelong friend, couldn't see through his clever masks.

Love stories? They're not to be found—except once. As a rule, Holmes had no time for romance. All his energies were needed for solving crimes. But in one story, a mysterious woman entered the picture. Her name was Irene Adler, but Holmes called her simply "the Woman." In spite of his single ways, Holmes fell for her. But was it real? Could she be trusted? Sorry, old bean. To find out what happens, you'll have to read "A Scandal in Bohemia."

The bad guys Holmes faced were worthy of his talents. Among them, Professor Moriarity stands out as the evil mastermind of all time. Moriarity was as good at crime as Holmes was at detection. He actually took Holmes—and himself—to his death in one story. During a fight they both fell over a cliff. But readers were upset to see the amazing detective die. So Doyle had to write another story bringing both men back to life! And Holmes lived on. His last story appeared in 1914, just as World War I was beginning.

Watson is the person who tells the stories. He became nearly as famous as Holmes himself. Long-winded and warm, he was everything the detective was not. He was also Holmes's truest friend. Watson's foolishness could even be helpful in solving crimes. By following the wrong clues, he sometimes gave Holmes an idea for catching the criminal.

A word about the "real" Holmes. It's true he had a curved pipe and often used a magnifying glass. But he did *not* wear the famous cap shown in many pictures, the one with a bill in front and another in back. That cap was worn by an actor who played Holmes on stage. Also, some of the things people *think* Holmes said were made up by actors who portrayed him on stage or in movies.

Doyle's stories first appeared in magazines. Then they were collected in books. After that, they were performed thousands of times on stage and in a long series of hit movies. In time they became the best-selling detective series ever. Around the world, "Sherlockian" clubs formed, and even today they continue to meet. The members reread and talk about the tales endlessly.

Believe it or not, some of the people who studied Holmes most carefully were real-life detectives! His methods actually changed the way police officers went about solving crimes.

The Case of the Dying Detective shows why interest in Holmes is still as keen as ever. The story opens as Watson is called to 221 Baker Street by Holmes's landlady, Mrs. Hudson. She says the detective is gravely ill. Watson hurries to Holmes's bedside and is shocked to find him near death. But Holmes won't let Watson treat him. Instead, he asks Watson to bring back a complete stranger—the one man in the whole world who can help.

As you read, be a detective yourself. Look for clues to the puzzle—and trust no one! At the story's end, you'll find that the answers have been right in front of you all along. "Just so," as Holmes might say.

—Chapter 2—

The End?

Imagine, if you can, my shock at reading the following message:

Dr. Watson, come at once. He's dying!

—Mrs. Hudson

I ran for my overcoat and bag. When my dear wife asked where I was going, I pressed the note into her hand. I could hear her gasp as I dashed out the front door.

It was a foul, foggy November night in London. I hailed a horse-drawn cab and jumped in. "Go to 221 Baker Street—and hurry!" I cried. Above the clattering of the horse's hooves, my mind raced.

Sherlock Holmes was dying. Was it possible?

Until my wedding two years ago, the great detective and I had been the best of partners. I'd followed him through all his famous cases: The Hound of the Baskervilles, the Sign of Four, the Speckled Band, and others.

Could the evil Professor Moriarity have caught up with him at last? No, I decided. Holmes was at home in his apartment. The place was carefully guarded by his Baker Street Irregulars, so no one could sneak in. I tapped on the cab roof with my walking stick. "Faster, please!" I called to the driver. The gaslights of London flew by the cab window.

Mrs. Hudson answered my knock at once. "Thank goodness you're here," she said. "Mr. Holmes has been sinking for nearly a week. I'm afraid he may not last the night!"

"Was there an accident?" I asked. "Has he been injured?"

"No, sir," she answered. "Some terrible sickness has got him. But he wouldn't let me call anybody. You know how pig-headed he can be!" She twisted a dishcloth in her hands and dabbed away a tear.

"As you know, sir, I serve him all his meals," she continued. "Well, for three days he wouldn't eat or drink a thing. But this morning I saw his face, with his cheeks all sunk in, and I could stand it no longer. 'With or without your leave, Mr. Holmes,' I told him, 'I am sending for a doctor!' "

"You are a kindly person, Mrs. Hudson. What was his answer?"

"He shook his head, kind of sad-like. 'Let it be Watson, then,' he said. And so I sent the note."

I hung my coat on a hook and, with fear in my heart, started up the stairs. His door was open. Inside, the lamp was low. In the dim light, I saw my friend in his bed.

Being a doctor, I had seen many sick people die. Even so, I let out a gasp at Holmes's appearance. His cheekbones stood out, casting dark shadows on his face. His eyes seemed to be burning with the brightness of fever. There was sweat upon his brow and dark crusts on his thin lips. His claw-like hands jerked and trembled. When at last he spoke, his voice rattled and croaked. He was but a shell of the man I knew.

"Watson," he said weakly, "it's good to see you again."

"My dear fellow!" I cried, nearing the bed.

"Stand back! Stand right back!" he said sharply. I drew back as if stung. "If you approach me, Watson, I shall order you out of the house."

"I only wished to help," I explained.

"Exactly! You will help best by doing what you are told."

"Certainly, Holmes."

He fell back on the pillow, heaving a great sigh. It pained me to see him so weak. I waited while he gathered his strength. Clearly, talking took a good deal out of him.

After a while he said, "I trust your dog is behaving himself after today's outdoor lunch?"

I blinked in amazement. Holmes and I had not spoken for weeks. Yet he knew what had happened to me only hours ago!

"Y-yes," I said, "he's fine now. But how on earth did you . . . ?"

Holmes waved away my words with the toss of a hand. "Surely anyone else would say the same," he said with a yawn. "The signs are so obvious. As you entered, I noticed a bit of dog hair on your jacket. Ordinarily you would have brushed it off. Then I saw you walking with a slight limp. I hope your knee is not hurt?"

"Uh, no," I mumbled. Holmes paused a moment to breathe, then continued speaking.

*"And finally, there is the matter of your slacks," he said. "The left leg has a small rip in it. It probably tore on a thorn. By any chance, was the dog chasing a skunk?"

"Exactly!" I replied. "I ordered him to stop, but he dashed off into the bushes. As I went after him, my leg caught on a bush. I tripped and bumped my knee. The skunk had better luck. The little stinker got away."

"Ah."

"But how did you know about the outdoor lunch?" I asked. Holmes did not reply. He simply glanced at my sleeve, which bore a fresh mustard stain.

I was glad to see that his astounding powers of observation were as keen as ever. But his appearance was truly alarming.

"I declare, Holmes," I said, "why must I remain across the room?"

"It's for your sake, Watson," he said.

"My sake?"

"Yes. I* seem to have picked up a rather bothersome little illness . . . while down by the city docks . . . about a week ago. . . ." His voice trailed off.

I shook my head. "Holmes, are you saying you were spending time at the docks? Why, all sorts of diseases enter London that way! Many of them we know nothing about."

My friend nodded slowly. "Just so, Doctor. One of the sailors told me what it was."

"What did he say?" I asked, opening my black bag. "Perhaps I have something for it."

Holmes answered with a word I could not understand. Then he smiled darkly. "The English name for it is the China flu," he croaked. "I assure you it is deadly—and very catching. So keep your distance if you care to go on living!"

"Now then, old man," I said, walking toward the bed. "I am a doctor, after all, and your dearest friend. I would never—"

"Mind me!" Holmes cried, sitting bolt upright in the bed. "Take not a step more!"

Seeing the terrible state he was in, I respected his wishes. He tottered a moment, then fixed his eyes on me with a steely look.

"Watson," he said in a low voice, "there is only one chance on earth my life can be saved. It is entirely up to you. You must do exactly as I say—immediately and without hesitation. If you cannot agree to do so, I must ask you to leave and not return."

His feverish eyes held me with a power I'd never seen before. Words failed me. I could only return his gaze and nod dumbly. When he was sure of my answer, he fell back on the pillow again, his last ounce of strength gone.

—Chapter 3—

The Box

Out of respect for Holmes, I always agreed to his demands—even when I least understood them. However, what he was about to ask would test me to the limit.

"See here, Holmes," I said. "You are not yourself. A sick man is but a child, and so I will treat you like a child. Whether you like it or not, I must see that you are under a doctor's care. Please let me help you."

My friend was slow in recovering his strength. "John," he said mildly, "I know you want the best for me. And I can see your feelings are hurt. For this I am sorry. But tell me, what do you know about the China flu?"

"Well," I replied, "I know the name, of course, but there is little about it in my medical books."

"I thought as much," Holmes said. His hands began to tremble again. "I have done some studies on disease, as you know."

"*Some* studies, Holmes? Why, you are regarded as England's leading expert in disease! Your paper on sleeping sickness was nothing short of brilliant."

The dying detective brushed my words aside. "Let us not waste words in idle chatter, Watson. I have done studies and learned much about my disease. Unfortunately, I was able to find no cure."

"But Holmes—we are in luck!" I cried. "It happens that Dr. William Aston, the greatest living expert on such diseases, is in London. I shall have him here within the hour!"

"Watson . . . ," my friend began. But I wasn't listening. Grabbing my bag, I turned to leave—only to find the door locked shut.

"Great Scott!" I exclaimed. "Mrs. Hudson has accidentally locked me in."

"Watson," Holmes repeated weakly, "Mrs. Hudson is not at fault. Please sit down and listen." He panted a little, and then he spoke again. "I know you sometimes act before thinking . . . so I had her set the latch . . . to lock as you entered the room. When you have heard . . . what I am about to say . . . I will tell you how to get out. . . ."

*Feeling a bit foolish, I put down my bag and took a seat. But Holmes spoke no more. His head slowly sagged onto the pillow.

"Holmes?"

In the near darkness I could hardly see his face. I turned up the lamp for a better look. All was well. His breathing was slow and regular. Having worn himself out, he was now sleeping. I settled back to wait.

As the minutes passed, I looked around the room. Holmes did not care about orderly surroundings, so his apartment was a mess. His overcoat hung on a peg. A bookshelf held his curved pipe and magnifying glass. On the desk were a handgun, a fingerprint brush, and other items.

I got up and started wandering around. Books, bottles, and test tubes littered his desk. Then a new object caught my eye. It was a tiny white box covered with a lovely design. I* was just opening the lid, when—

"STOP!!"

21

I jumped at the sound of Holmes's voice. I turned around and was startled to see him kneeling on the bed, holding up a hand.

I removed my hand from the lid.

"Now put it down—*gently*," he said. I did so.

"Look here, Holmes—what's the meaning of this?" I demanded.

He remained kneeling, bracing himself with both arms. I could see how hard this was for him, so I sat down again, as near to the bed as I dared come.

"What's in that box, Holmes?" I asked. "You look as if you'd seen a ghost."

"I very nearly did," he mumbled, more to himself than to me. He lay back. "Forgive me, Watson. I must have nodded off." A confused look crossed his face and he rubbed his brow. "I was about to . . . to tell you. . . ."

"Indeed you were, Holmes," I said. "You were about to explain how I might help you, and how to unlock this door!"

"Ah, yes." His eyes became sharp again, though his voice was now weaker than ever. "You must not go for Dr. Aston, Watson. I am certain he could do me no good. There is but one man in the entire world who can help me."

"Name him and I'll be off," I said.

"Those are the first intelligent words you have spoken since you arrived, Watson. I knew I could rely on you."

"Thank you, Holmes. Again I ask, what is this gentleman's name?"

The sharpness faded from his eyes. "What gentleman?" he asked weakly.

"Why, the man you need, Holmes!"

"Oh . . . oh yes, of course," he said, reaching into the night-table drawer for a notepad. "Here is his name and where he lives." He wrote for a moment, and then he stopped.

He opened the drawer of the night table again and pulled out a thick glove. He tossed the glove to me and said, "Watson, kindly pick up that box . . . with this . . . and put them both into the desk."

Seeing his strength failing again, I hurried to do his bidding. I carefully placed the box in the center drawer along with the glove. When I turned to Holmes again, he was staring dully at the floor.

"May I have the address, Holmes? *Holmes?*"

He jumped, as if aroused from sleep. "Yes, Watson," he answered carelessly, crushing his note into a ball and tossing it in my direction. "Oh, I need something else from you."

"Name it, Holmes," I said, leaning in to hear him.

"You must return to me before he does. Do not come back together—is that clear?"

"Of course, if you wish," I answered. Then Holmes's expression changed.

"Tell me, old man, do you have any money on you? Any coins, that is?" he asked.

"Well, I usually have a few pennies," I answered, fishing through my pockets. "Yes, here are seven pennies. But why?"

When I looked up, Holmes was smiling cheerfully. "Be good enough to put them under that plant, would you?" Wondering what this could mean, I did so. Holmes sank into the pillow again, still smiling.

I smoothed out the note and tried to read Holmes's writing. "The man in question is Mr. Culver Smith of 411 King's Cross Road. Is that right, Holmes?"

"I suppose so," he replied aimlessly. Did he know what I was saying? I began to wonder.

"Now, Holmes, you must tell me how to get out," I said. To my alarm, he laughed loudly.

"Why, you goose, it's easy! Press that button—just there—while turning the latch. Really, old fellow, a child could do it!"

I got the door open and turned to him. "But, Holmes, what about that little white box?" I asked. "What was inside it?"

Holmes's red-rimmed eyes grew wide. "Box? What box? I don't see any box."

With my heart racing, I hurried into the hall.

—Chapter 4—

The Visit

Mrs. Hudson was waiting for me in the hall. I could see she had been crying.

"Oh, Dr. Watson, how is he? Will he last through the night?" she asked.

"There, there, Mrs. Hudson. Please don't worry. Mr. Holmes is resting now. I'm going to bring someone who can help him."

"I hope he's a nice chap," she said. "As you know, Dr. Watson, you sometimes bring some pretty strange fellows up here."

I had to admit she was right. During my partnership with the great detective, I had met some very shady people. "Rest assured, I will bring no criminals here tonight," I said. "I am off to find Mr. Smith, as Holmes has asked. Thank you, Mrs. Hudson, for looking after our dear friend."

*Out on the street, I headed for the corner to hail a cab. Then I heard a young voice whisper my name.

"Over here, Dr. Watson!"

In the shadow of a low-hanging tree I could see the outline of a girl. Then I remembered her voice.

"Janie, is that you?" I asked, joining her in the darkness.

Janie Claire was one of the Baker Street Irregulars. Some time before, Holmes had saved the lives of several homeless children. Some evil men had tried to catch them and sell them as slaves. The men went to prison, but they said they would get even with Holmes. Ever since then, on dark nights, Janie and her friends stood guard over his apartment.

"How's he doing?" she asked.

"He is holding his own," I answered, "and I'm on my way to get help." As I turned to go, the girl grabbed my sleeve.*

"Watch out!" she warned. She pointed to a place down the block. "There's a man hiding in that doorway. He's been here for hours."

"Thank you, Janie. I'll take care. But now I must be off."

I hurried away down the block. As I neared the doorway, the hidden man stepped into the light. I knew him instantly.

"Police Inspector Morton!" I said. "What brings you out on such a cold night?" The man was Reggie Morton, an officer from Scotland Yard. He was dressed in ordinary clothes, not his official suit. But under one arm I thought I saw the outline of a gun.

"I might ask you the same question," the burly fellow said. "You've been to see Mr. Sherlock Holmes, is that right?"

Holmes and I had worked with Morton on a case several years ago. I knew him to be rather slow, but he was brave in a fight. "Holmes is not well," I said.

Morton squinted for a second. Was he surprised? In the dim lamplight I couldn't tell.

"Is he in danger?" Morton asked.

"Well, yes, but not from criminals," I replied. Just then an empty cab passed by. "Ho! You there! Hold your horse!" I cried, chasing after it. Seconds later I jumped aboard and gave the driver Smith's address.

As the cab clattered along, I tried to understand the strange events of the night. I wondered why Holmes was keeping me, a trained doctor, at a distance. Why had he asked me to put the coins under the plant? I recalled his laughter when I couldn't open the door— quite unlike him, really. And with a chill in my heart, I remembered his words, "Box? What box? I don't see any box." Had the disease affected his mind? Was he losing his grip on reality? Was the world's most brilliant mind slipping into madness?

Fortunately there was little time for such grim thoughts. Smith's home was only minutes away. It was a large, gloomy-looking house in an upper-class part of town. It even had electric lighting, the cost of which was beyond the means of ordinary people. I was not surprised when a butler answered the bell.

"My name is Dr. John Watson," I told the butler, presenting my card.

"Is Mr. Smith expecting you?" he asked slowly.

"No. But I am here on a matter of some urgency. I must speak with him immediately."

The long-faced butler examined my card at length. "I shall see if he can speak with you. Kindly wait here," he said. Then he turned and walked to a door down the hallway, knocked, and entered.

For many years my name had been linked with Holmes's. Owing to his fame, I was well known to the people of London—and, indeed, the world. But from the sound of Smith's voice, I could tell he knew nothing of me.

"Who is this person?" Smith demanded. "What does he want? I am not to be disturbed during my hours of study. Dear me, James, how often have I told you that?"

I heard the butler give some reply.

"Well, I won't see him, James. Say I am not at home. Tell him to come back in the morning."

I thought of Holmes tossing upon his bed of sickness. Surely he was counting the minutes until I could bring help. This was a time for quick action. His very life depended on me. Good manners be hanged—I *would* see Mr. Smith!

As James returned, I pushed past him and burst into the office. With a cry of protest, Smith rose from a chair near the fireplace. He had a great yellow face, bushy eyebrows, and a strong jaw. His hard gray eyes glared at me. A colorful Chinese nightcap covered his hairless head.

A second look revealed something else. Although his head was large, his body was small and weak. My doctor's eye noticed he was twisted in the shoulders and back. Perhaps he had been sick as a child.

"What's this?" Smith cried in a high voice. "How dare you break into my office!"

"Sir, I am sorry to force myself upon you," I replied. "But this is a very serious matter. Sherlock Holmes—"

My friend's name had an amazing effect on the little man. Rage instantly left his face and was replaced by keen interest.

"Have you come from Holmes?" he asked quickly.

"I have just left him."

"What about Holmes? How is he?"

"He is gravely sick. That is why I have come."

The man showed me to a chair and then sat again in his own. As he turned away, I caught sight of his face in the mirror. For a split second he seemed to be wearing an evil smile. But I told myself that could not be. Holmes had asked for Smith. And in his weakened state, Holmes would be helpless against anyone meaning him harm.

In any case, Smith looked at me with real concern. "I am sorry to hear this," he said. "I know Holmes only from some friends we have in common. But I read newspaper stories of his work, of course. And I have only the highest regard for his ability."

"Holmes said you alone could help him. Are you a medical doctor?" I asked.

"Not exactly," Smith replied, smoothing the robe he was wearing. "But I am interested in disease, just as Holmes is interested in crime. These are some of the criminals I have caught." He pointed to shelves lining the wall.

On them lay bottles, jars, test tubes, a microscope, and other laboratory equipment. "In these bottles, some of the world's worst killers are serving time." It chilled me to think of the danger the bottles contained.

"But tell me," he went on, "why does Holmes think I can be of help?"

"He said you were an expert in diseases from the East," I replied. Smith nodded. I continued, "Holmes became sick while working among sailors down at the docks. He believes he has the China flu."

"He does, does he?" Smith asked, rubbing his stubby fingers together. "Perhaps things are not as bad as they seem. How long has he been sick?"

"About three days."

"What about his mind?" Smith asked carefully. "Is he thinking clearly?"

"For a while he was. But as I was about to leave, he . . . well, he wasn't himself. Please, sir, I beg you to come!"

"By all means, Dr. Watson. It would be wrong not to help a dying man. I shall come with you at once. Give me a moment or two to dress."

Reaching for my bag, I remembered what Holmes had said.

"Holmes was very afraid I might catch his illness," I said. "He asked that you come alone." I wrote Holmes's address on a card and handed it to Smith.

"Very well, then," Smith said. "James will show you out, and I shall visit Mr. Holmes within the next half hour."

Once outside, I lost no time in hailing a cab. My task was done well. Now, I wondered, would Smith do his?

—Chapter 5—

The Truth

As the cab neared the corner of Baker Street, I asked the driver to let me off. After paying my fare I walked quickly down the dimly lighted sidewalk. I stopped in front of the bushes where Janie had been before.

I looked into the shadows, but I saw nothing. Just then a voice behind me spoke.

"Looking for me?"

I nearly jumped out of my skin. The voice belonged to Janie, of course. "My dear girl," I said, "you gave me such a fright! Now listen carefully, because there's no time to lose. Mr. Holmes is expecting another visitor, who should be here at any moment. You must let him in immediately. This may be Holmes's last chance!"

"If anyone but you had said that, I would think he was pulling a fast one," Janie said. "But for you, I'll tell the others to let him pass." She turned and hooted like an owl. Answering hoots came from other parts of the block. "You can go in now, Doc."

Mrs. Hudson met me at the door. "At last!" she cried, taking my coat. "It seems like hours since you left. But where's your Mr. Smith?"

"He'll be along directly. Has there been any change?"

"I'm very worried, Dr. Watson. I haven't heard a peep from upstairs since you left."

Fighting panic, I hurried up to Holmes's apartment.

His door stood open, but I hesitated. For all I knew, the worst had come to pass. I stepped in and turned up the lamp. But a welcome surprise awaited me.

"Watson, old fellow—how nice to see you again!" Holmes said.

He still looked like someone at death's door, but he appeared to be feeling better. His voice was strong, and his eyes were clear. I smiled with relief as he sat up.

"Well, did you see him, Watson?" Holmes asked.

"Yes. He will be here any minute."

"Excellent. Did he ask what was wrong with me?"

"I told him about the China flu and how you caught it."

"Exactly! Well, Watson, you have done all a good friend could. But now I must ask for one final favor."

"I am at your service," I said.

"You must disappear."

"Holmes, you're not sending me away! I want to see what Smith has to say."

"And so do I, my friend," Holmes said with a slight smile. "I simply meant you must hide yourself while he's here. I believe he will speak more frankly if he thinks he and I are alone."

I was used to Holmes's odd requests, but this one struck me as nearly impossible. I looked wonderingly around the one-room apartment.

"But there's no closet," I said. "Where could I hide?"

"There's just enough room behind my bed. First put your bag and coat under the desk."

"Now see here, Holmes—this is most irregular!"

"That's the way, old fellow," Holmes said as I hid my coat and medical bag under the desk.

"But, Holmes, I feel like a common robber!"

"Even so, Watson, this is absolutely . . . wait! I hear a cab." To my amazement, Holmes sprang out of bed and peeked between the shades. "It's him. We haven't a moment to lose. Quickly!"

Feeling like a perfect fool, I got on my hands and knees and crawled behind the bed. I heard Holmes jump back under the covers.

"Now, Watson," he whispered, "you must remain there, no matter what happens. Don't speak! Don't move! Just listen with all your ears." He turned the lamp down and lay still, as before.

Seconds later, Mrs. Hudson let Smith in.

From my hiding place I could hear the door open and close. Then came Smith's footsteps crossing the room. In the quiet, I could also hear Holmes's gasping breath. Had he taken a turn for the worse? I peeked cautiously around the bedpost.

Smith was standing at Holmes's bedside, looking at him.

"Holmes," he said. "Holmes!" He bent down and shook him. "Can't you hear me? Wake up, I say!"

The dying detective slowly opened his eyes. "Is that you, Mr. Smith?" he whispered. "I hardly dared hope you would come."

Smith laughed. "I hardly thought you would ask for me," he said. "And yet, here we are."

"It is very good of you—very fine, really," Holmes said. This brought a snicker from Smith.

"So you're glad to see me," Smith said. "That's odd. The last time we spoke you were trying to put me behind bars. Or don't you remember that?"

"Of course I do," Holmes replied thickly. "Victor Savage had died by your hand. He said you had stolen his plans . . . and I knew it was true. Please, Smith . . . get me . . . some water."

"Not just yet," Smith said. He took the pitcher off the table and began watering the plants. I fought the urge to step forth and shake him.

"No, Holmes, your memory must be failing. I never killed Victor Savage. He died of the China flu. Dr. Watson says you have it too. It's funny, isn't it? Only two cases of the China flu in all of London—his and yours," Smith said, laughing scornfully.

"You're the only man . . . who knows the cure," Holmes gasped. "Please . . ."

"Oh, stop!" Smith growled. "Don't expect help from someone you called a killer. And anyway, there is no cure for the China flu. How long have you had it?"

"Three . . . days," Holmes croaked.

"Then you haven't much longer to live. Victor Savage lasted only four days, and he was younger and stronger than you. Smarter, too, if you ask me! Your friend Watson said you caught it at the docks."

"Are you saying . . . it came from somewhere else?" Holmes asked.

Smith started to say something. Then he stopped. He twirled his watch on its chain and smiled. "I must say, Holmes, I expected more from the world's greatest detective. First you failed to prove I killed Victor Savage. Now you fail to find the cause of your *own* death." He walked about the room, poking at Holmes's belongings. "What a lot of clobber!" Smith cried. "Too bad you'll never see my place, where a *real* scientist works."

"So, Smith," Holmes panted, "do you admit . . . you killed Savage?"

"I admit nothing!" Smith snapped. "Really, Holmes, I'm surprised. You've dogged my trail for years. By now you should know my habits. Do you suppose I would let down my guard just because you're dying?"

Holmes groaned, sinking lower in the bed.

*As for me, I could stand it no longer. This fellow, who surely had robbed and killed another man, was killing Holmes as well. And like a cat with a mouse, he was making a game out of it! Forgetting my promise, I burst out of my hiding place with a wild yell.

Being somewhat heavier than Smith, I found him hard to catch. He ran to the fireplace and grabbed the poker. Now I was the one being chased!

I knew Holmes had a collection of walking sticks near the window. As I pulled one out, Smith swung the poker. Luckily, he misjudged the distance. An inch closer and it might have been the end of me!

I raised my stick. Smith dropped the poker and ran for the door. It was locked, as before. I chased him this way and that, sending books and jars crashing to the* floor. But suddenly Smith stopped me in my tracks. He had found Holmes's gun—and was pointing it straight at me!

"Don't move, Watson," Holmes said tightly. He had left the bed and now stood beside me. Seeing him up close, I noticed odd things. The shadows on his cheeks were drawn with pencil. Bits of beeswax hung from his lips. His forehead was smeared with oil that looked like sweat. And red coloring made his eyes seem bloodshot. His illness had been a disguise!

Now the two of us were at gunpoint. However, the noise had brought Mrs. Hudson—and someone else.

"Inspector Morton!" I cried. "What luck that you were passing by. You're just in time to arrest this dangerous killer!"

"Not so fast!" Smith warned, waving the gun. Everyone froze. I waited tensely, wondering who would be shot first. Smith made up his mind. But no shots came. Instead, he did the last thing in the world I expected. Smiling, he handed the gun over to Holmes!

—Chapter 6—

The Unmasking

For a moment that seemed like an hour, no one moved.

There we stood: Holmes, holding his gun; I, watching Smith; Mrs. Hudson, wondering what had happened; Morton, guarding the door; and the criminal himself, still smiling.

"Well, look at us," Smith said. "Like actors in a play. It's Act Three, and we're all on stage together. But this time there's no happy ending. The great detective has solved no crimes!"

"Don't be too sure of yourself, Smith," I said. "From my hiding place I heard everything you said. You might as well have admitted you killed Victor Savage!"

"Wait a minute, you two," Morton said, moving between us. "Will someone tell me what's going on here?"

"I think I can shed some light on this," Holmes said, slipping the gun into a drawer and locking it.

"Mr. Holmes—you're well again!" Mrs. Hudson cried. "Dr. Watson, how did you work such a wonder?"

"There is much to thank the good doctor for," Holmes said, smiling. "But in fact I needed no help. You see, I never really had the China flu."

"But I saw you, Mr. Holmes," the landlady said. "You never left this apartment. Day after day you had no food or water. I saw you get worse by the hour. Even now—"

Holmes interrupted her. "Please don't upset yourself, Mrs. Hudson." He took a cloth from the wash stand, wet it, and rubbed his face. Everyone gasped in surprise. He was thinner than usual, certainly. But the shadows on his cheeks came off. So did the redness around his eyes. He brushed away the beeswax on his lips. In seconds, he was the Holmes we knew.

*"I'm sorry for having fooled you—and you as well, Watson. But you see, I was setting a trap. I had to make you think I was dying. If you did not believe, you would not have played your parts so well. And we would never have caught this snake!"

"Call me names if you want to, Holmes," Smith said. "You still haven't proven anything."

"I'll get around to you in a moment," Holmes said coolly. "First I must answer Inspector Morton's question."

"Indeed so, Mr. Holmes. And it had better make sense. I've been standing across the street all evening, and I'm frozen stiff!" Morton said.

"Mrs. Hudson," Holmes said, glancing at the clock, "I believe you've put water on for tea. By now it should be at the boil. Would you be good enough to get us all a nice, large pot?"

"Why, certainly, sir. But how on* earth did you know the water was boiling?"

"I have observed that you are very regular in your habits," Holmes said, pulling his chair up to the table. "You always take tea just before retiring."

"Well, I never . . . ," the good woman mumbled, heading for the door.

"Oh—and please bring along some of your little sandwiches," Holmes added. "I believe we're all a bit hungry."

"On with your story, please," Morton said

Holmes put his fingertips together. "It all began with the Victor Savage case," he said. "Do you remember that one, Inspector?"

"I should say so," Morton answered. "I was there when the judge let Smith go."

"Then I'll explain for Dr. Watson, who was getting married just then. He may have missed reading about it." I nodded. "You see," Holmes continued, "Savage and Smith were partners in a company. They sold those new things people are all listening to these days. I can never remember what they're called. . . ."

"Radios," Smith said dryly.

"Ah, yes," Holmes said. "Well, Smith owned a small part of the company, but Savage was the brains behind it. Savage had invented a new device that was worth millions. But if he died, Smith could take over everything. And in fact, Savage did die—"

"Of the China flu," Smith said, finishing Holmes's sentence.

"Exactly. And it just so happens that you, Smith, are an expert in the China flu."

Smith smiled scornfully. "It was just his bad luck. The judge said so!"

"But see here!" I cried. "You all but admitted you gave Holmes the same disease. I heard you!"

"Did you?" Smith asked, looking me in the face. "Think carefully. Did I say so—in those very words?"

I fumbled for a reply.

"I'm sorry, Dr. Watson," Morton said, "but he's right. It may have *sounded* like an admission that he killed Savage. But unless he said it straight out, I can't arrest him."

"Holmes," I said, "didn't he say it?"

The detective frowned. "I'm afraid not, old man. My plan was to trick him into doing so. But you jumped out before I could finish."

"Then I'm free to go!" Smith cried, picking up his coat.

"Yes, but do have a cup of tea first," Holmes said agreeably. "Here's Mrs. Hudson now."

"No, thanks," Smith said. "I'm off—and you'll never see me again!"

I wanted to yell, "Stop that killer!" or stop him myself. But Holmes remained as cool as ever.

"Before you go, Smith," he said, "I have something of yours." Smith stopped while Holmes reached into the desk.

"You left something here last week," he said, taking out the glove and slipping it on. "You may need this in your laboratory." His gloved hand pulled the white box from the drawer where I had placed it.

"You see," Holmes explained to us, "this pretty little thing was how Smith planned to do away with me. I haven't looked inside, of course. I must be careful about unexpected gifts."

"Indeed he is," Mrs. Hudson said. "He wouldn't even let me touch it."

"But, Holmes, how do you know what's inside?" Morton asked.

"I don't, actually—but I have a very strong hunch. My hunch is that under the lid is a strong spring. On the spring is a sharp point. And on that point is a coating of the China flu."

"Of course!" I cried. "As the lid is lifted, the spring pops out, and the point sticks the finger of the person holding the box." Again fear went up my spine. "Had it stuck me, I would have caught the China flu. That's why you made me wear a glove!"

"A clever device, is it not?" Holmes asked. "The holder throws the box into the trash, leaving no clue to the crime. The tiny mark from the point heals over, but a few days later the person is dead."

"You're mad!" Smith yelled. "That's an ordinary box. And even it if *is* a trick box, you can't pin it on me!"

"No? Well, what if the China flu *is* inside? And what if I—the only other man besides Savage—were to die from it? You have good reason to want me dead. Would any judge believe that you—an expert—were not the sender?"

Smith began backing up.

"But don't worry, Smith," Holmes said. "There is a simple way to prove your innocence." He held the box up to Smith's face. "Open it!"

Smith drew back as if the box had fangs. Then he abruptly turned and dashed out the door Mrs. Hudson had left open.

"After him!" I cried. Morton and I charged toward the door, but Holmes sat down quietly. A smile played upon his lips.

A second later I understood why. From the hall came footsteps and voices, an instant of silence, and a loud bumping noise. We burst through the doorway. There, at the top of the stairs, stood Janie and another girl. At the bottom lay Smith, holding his head.

"Hey, your lordship— did you enjoy your trip?" Janie called to Smith. We all joined in a hearty laugh.

Half an hour later, Smith was safely behind bars. Mrs. Hudson had gone to bed. And Holmes and I were enjoying a meal at an all-night restaurant.

"Holmes," I said, "you've eaten everything but the dishes!"

"So I have," he said, sitting back. "Three days without food and water does put an edge on the appetite."

"Was that really needed?" I asked. "You might have starved."

"I was in no danger, really," he replied. "But I had to be sure you and Mrs. Hudson were fooled, or you could never have fooled Smith."

"Yes, but please don't do that again, old boy. I'm still shaking from the fright you gave me! And wasn't it lucky that Inspector Morton happened to be nearby?"

"Not exactly luck, Watson. I had sent him a note telling him to watch for trouble. I knew Mrs. Hudson would send for you, so I asked him to be on guard tonight."

"Holmes, I know I'm a bit thick-headed, but how did you know it was Smith who sent that box?"

Holmes toyed for a moment with his water glass. "You know, of course, that I never leave a case unsolved. However long it may take, I always get my man."

"Yes, quite," I said.

"Smith knew this too. As you could see, he's no fool. He must have known I would continue to hunt him. And of course he was right. That's why I was studying the China flu. But his sending the box was very clever."

"You seemed to know quite a lot about that little trick," I observed.

"For many years I have been exchanging letters with another detective in the East. He once wrote me about a box very much like the one Smith sent."

I shook my head. "You never fail to astound me. Who else but Sherlock Holmes would know about a deadly trick invented half a world away?"

"Tut-tut, Watson," he answered. "It's all in a day's work. It's *you* who should be taking a bow. After all, you played your part like a professional actor. And for that I am deeply grateful, old friend. Bravo!"

I raised my hand to call the waiter.

"Another plate of chops, please," I said. "And don't spare the onions."